MARK TWAIN and the

Queens of the MISSISSIPPI

CHERYL HARNESS

SIMON & SCHUSTER BOOKS FOR YOUNG READERS

SIMON & SCHUSTER BOOKS FOR YOUNG READERS
An imprint of Simon & Schuster Children's Publishing Division
1230 Avenue of the Americas   New York, New York 10020
Copyright © 1998 by Cheryl Harness

Book design by Anahid Hamparian
The text for this book is set in 15-point Charlotte.
The illustrations are rendered in watercolor and colored pencil.
Printed and bound in the United States of America
First Edition

10 9 8 7 6 5 4 3 2 1
Library of Congress Cataloging-in-Publication Data
Harness, Cheryl.
Mark Twain and the queens of the Mississippi / written and illustrated by Cheryl Harness.
p.   cm.
Includes bibliographical references.
Summary: Focuses on this American author's connection with steamboats on the Mississippi River while also presenting a history of the craft.
ISBN 0-689-81542-5
1. Twain, Mark, 1835–1916—Homes and haunts—Mississippi River—Juvenile literature. 2. Authors, American, 19th century—Biography—Juvenile literature.
3. Steamboats—Mississippi River—History—Juvenile literature. [1. Twain, Mark, 1835–1910—Homes and haunts.
2. Authors, American. 3. Steamboats. 4. Mississippi River.] I. Title.
PS1334.H37 1998
818'.409—dc21
[B]
97-40799

For Laura and for Chris

To the river of rivers and its people I say thanks.
Look for higher ground in April;
Stand in reverence on its banks.

$\mathscr{A}$UTHOR'S $\mathscr{N}$OTE

**The Mississippi is well worth reading about. It is not a
commonplace river, but on the contrary is in all ways remarkable**.
MARK TWAIN: *Life on the Mississippi*

Samuel Clemens, known to the world as Mark Twain, the author, thought the Mississippi River was well worth writing about. And no one wrote about it better than he did, especially in his books about Tom Sawyer and his friend Huckleberry Finn.

Mark Twain based the adventures of Tom and Huck on his own adventures growing up in the village of Hannibal, Missouri, on the bank of the Mississippi River at a glorious time in the river's history. The river was nineteenth-century America's Main Street. It was crowded with all kinds of people-powered rafts and boats. Then, as a comet streaked across the sky and the earth quaked, steam came to the river in 1811. Steam-powered paddleboats reigned up and down the river. Twenty-four years later, another comet was seen in the sky and Sam Clemens was born. I'm sure it was just a coincidence.

THE MISSISSIPPI RIVER begins small, in northern Minnesota. But further along, tons of washed-away soil, melting snow, and groundwater from a wide basin of 1,247,300 square miles—almost half of the continental United States—drain into creeks, streams, and rivers, which in turn flow into the biggest river, the muddy "father of waters" of North America. Glaciers dug it mostly one hundred feet deep, nearly two million years ago. The Mississippi is widest at Cairo, Illinois: 4,500 feet. By the time it gets to the swampy country at the Gulf of Mexico, "Old Man River" has traveled 2,348 miles.

MARIAS
MILK
MUSSELSHELL
YELLOWSTONE
BIGHORN
COLUMBIA
SNAKE
COLORADO
LITTLE COLORADO
GILA
SALT
GILA

PACIFIC OCEAN

The river got its name from the tribes of people living on its banks thousands of years ago. They called themselves Chippewa, Missouri, Fox, Shawnee, Choctaw, Illinois, and many more. They called the wide moving waters *Mississippi*, meaning big river.

As far back as three thousand years ago, people in the valleys of the Mississippi and the Ohio Rivers were building big burial mounds, and the river people built some of North America's first cities, such as Cahokia in what is now called Illinois.

They hollowed out logs with fire and knives to make dugouts that floated on the water so they could fish and travel to trade with other tribes along the rivers. With tree bark or animal skin on bowed branches they made fine light canoes.

Over many years and miles, the kings of Europe sent men such as Hernando de Soto of Spain and Sieur de la Salle of France to explore this country they called America. Maybe they'd find gold, or a shortcut to India or China. The explorers told the river people that the land belonged to the kings now. Life was going to be different: Lots more people were going to be coming out of the east into the west.

The Mississippi rolled on, icy in the winters, rising in the springs, looping, shifting, now to the east, now to the west. Flatboats, broadhorns, skiffs, keelboats, rafts, and pirogues full of all kinds of people and cargo floated on the rippling water-road.

A long-tailed comet was seen in the heavens night after night the year when the Mississippi River ran backwards from the force of the terrible NEW MADRID EARTHQUAKE 1811, the year when steam came to the river.

Missouri RIVER

St. Louis

ILLINOIS Territory

INDIANA Territory

OHIO RIVER, Louisville

New Madrid

KENTUCKY

MISSISSIPPI RIVER

Natchez

PENELORE! (fire canoe!)

January 12, 1812
The Roosevelts arrive at
New Orleans

Nicholas and Lydia ROOSEVELT

Mr. Roosevelt's great-grand-nephew Theodore was to be 26th president of the United States.

1787~ on the Delaware River~ John Fitch launched America's first steam-driven boat. Later that year, James Rumsey built a faster one (three miles per hour) and sailed it up the Potomac River.

Robert Fulton's CLERMONT was the first commercially successful steamboat. She chugged, 5 miles per hour, up the HUDSON RIVER AUGUST 17, 1807. Mr. Fulton designed the New Orleans.

Then, in the fall of 1811, a new kind of boat appeared on the river for the first time: a steamboat. Water bubbled in a boiler over a fire. Steam from the boiling water drove an engine that turned a paddle wheel that pushed against the river. Vessels powered by steam could navigate down and *up* the river without having to be rowed, or towed, or moved by strong-armed men pushing poles with all their mights against the river bottom.

Young pioneers Nicholas and Lydia Roosevelt, their dog, and their crew set out in their steamboat, *New Orleans*, from Pittsburgh, Pennsylvania, on the Ohio River. The Mississippi greeted them with a big, blasting earthquake. Flocks of frightened birds darkened the sky. Terrified animals and people fled to the river where islands sank to the treetops and chunks of riverbank crashed away. New islands were shoved up from the muddy bottom as the Roosevelts' boat puffed along like a bobbing teakettle down the roiling, rushing, muddy rumpus to the sea.

Thirty years later, more than four hundred steamboats were puffing alongside the people-powered vessels on the Mississippi River and its tributaries. Where the native people had farmed and traded, villages of newcomers were growing along the river. The Indians were moved west from their valleys, whether they wanted to go or not.

Halley's Comet streaked across the sky when Samuel Langhorne Clemens was born in the village of Florida, Missouri November 30, 1835.

St. Paul
Minneapolis
Winona
La Crosse
Galena
Dubuque
Davenport
Rock Island
ILLINOIS
Burlington
Nauvoo
DES MOINES
Keokuk
Quincy
Hannibal
Alton
Cairo
Florida
St. Louis
New Madrid
OHIO
MISSOURI
Memphis
Helena
MISSISSIPPI
Vicksburg
Natchez
Baton Rouge

New Orleans

In one of these river towns there lived a small boy named Samuel,
Judge Clemens's boy. The best and liveliest time for Sam or anybody else
in his little town of Hannibal, Missouri, was when a sharp-eyed fellow
perched high on a bluff would sing out, "Ste-e-e-e-amboat's a'comin!"

Black smoke shot up out of the decorated smokestacks as passengers leaned on the lacy deck railings on either side of the brightly painted paddle box. Highest of all, on the "texas" deck, was the glittering glass pilothouse where the far-seeing, all-knowing pilot stood at the great wheel of his fiery-furnaced marvel.

Children ran past shopkeepers buttoning their waistcoats. Who's arrived? Did their shipment come? Sam and his friends envied the deckhands who yelled and cussed as they worked. If only they could talk like that! Soon, with a ringing of bells, the boat was on its way upriver to St. Paul or down to "St. Looey," looking like a floating wedding cake.

Sam stared longingly at the receding boat, wishing he could go along. He'd rather be a steamboatman than a clown, a king, or even a pirate with pockets full of gold doubloons!

EULA BELLE

13.

19.

16.

17.

1. **SMOKESTACKS** (or **CHIMNEYS**) Often their tops are cut to look like a crown of flames or feathers.
2. The **PILOT** is in charge of steering the boat at the big wheel in the **PILOT HOUSE** which sits high atop
3. The **TEXAS** which sits on top of
4. The **HURRICANE DECK** on top of
5. The **BOILER DECK** where passengers promenade above
6. The **MAIN DECK**
7. The **CAPTAIN** (who also may be the owner) is the boss on the boat. The clerk is the business manager and the engineer keeps the
8. **FURNACE, BOILER,** and the **ENGINES** going.
9. The **MATE** bosses the
10. **ROUSTABOUTS** who handle the cargo.
11. **JACK·STAFF**
12. **SPARS**
13. **STEAM ESCAPE VALVES**
14. **CAPSTAN**
15. The **BOW**
16. The **RUDDER** is at the **STERN**
17. The **PADDLE·BOX** houses the **PADDLE·WHEEL:** one on each side
18. **MAIN STAIRWAY**
19. **LIFEBOAT** or "**YAWL**"
20. The **HULL** is not as deep and round as on the Roosevelts' boat, the *New Orleans*, which was designed for the deep eastern rivers. The Mississippi and the other rivers of the west could be very shallow, so the **HULL** (the boat's bottom) had to be shallow too. This "engine on a raft" idea was thought of by **CAPTAIN HARRY SHREVE** in 1816.

But a different profession was waiting for Sam. In 1846, his father died. Eleven-year-old Sam was apprenticed to a printer: He would learn a trade in return for his keep. He earned his living in print shops and newspaper offices around the country east of the Mississippi for the next ten years, until the day he read about an expedition in the Amazon jungle. Young Sam's adventuring heart went thumping. "I'll be a *traveler*," he said to himself. The word had a satisfactory magic in it. He boarded the *Paul Jones*, a shabby old steamboat bound from Cincinnati to New Orleans, on April 15, 1857.

By the time he got to New Orleans, twenty-one-year-old Sam had changed his mind. His boyhood ambition was on fire again. Before the *Paul Jones* steamed back upriver to St. Louis, Sam had talked the pilot, Horace Bixby, into "learning" him the river. Young Sam Clemens would be a cub-pilot, a steamboatman at last.

Sam supposed that all a pilot had to do was to keep his boat in the wide river. How hard could that be? But he soon found out that beneath the shimmery top of the river lurked all kinds of dangers waiting to bash a boat's brains out: sandbars, dead trees, rocks, and boat wrecks. A pilot had to "read" the face of the water: How it looked told what it was hiding. He had to know the changing shape of the troublesome river upstream *and* down, every bend, every plantation, town, and island by heart so he could steer in inky dark or fog or moonlight and not bump the boat into the bank or the bottom.

Sam stood at the side of the big pilotwheel as was customary. "I haven't got brains enough to be a pilot; and if I had I wouldn't have strength enough to carry them around!" he exclaimed to Mr. Bixby.

"When I say I'll learn a man the river, I mean it," said Mr. Bixby. "You can depend upon it."

Sam learned all 1,300 miles of the lower Mississippi, all the way from St. Louis to New Orleans. Other pilots specialized in the upper river—from St. Louis to St. Paul. Sam received his pilot's certificate on April 9, 1859. To be a pilot, Sam thought proudly, was to be the only unfettered and entirely independent human being on earth. When he visited Hannibal, Sam pretended not to notice the admiring stares of the hometown boys and girls.

From his lofty pilothouse, Sam saw all kinds of rivercrafts: stern-wheelers whose one paddle wheel was at the back, log rafts, and side-wheeler packets. He saw flatboats heading south with the current and showboats and circus barges. Ferries carried people across the bridgeless Mississippi River.

MISSISSIPPI St.LOUIS RIVER CAIRO

MISSOURI RIVER

ISLAND No.10
was a rebel stronghold until
April 7, 1862. Now the U.S.
forces controlled the
river south to

MEMPHIS which
fell to U.S.
gunboats.

June 6, 1862

U.S. General
Ulysses S. Grant

The Civil War ended Sam's pilot days in the spring of 1861. Battles and blockades ended regular shipping on the Mississippi River. Sam was ordered to pilot "ironclad" gunboats for the Union but he did not want to fight against his home state of Missouri, whose governor sided with the South. He drilled for a while with a band of pro-South volunteers, but unhappy, out-of-a-job Sam didn't really want to fight the Union soldiers of the U. S. Government either, so when his big brother, Orion, asked him to go west with him, Sam left the river and the war behind. "I retired to private life, to give the Union cause a chance," said Sam wryly.

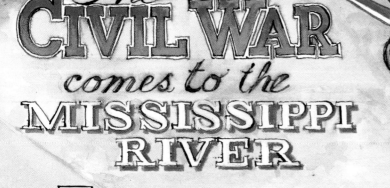

The CIVIL WAR comes to the MISSISSIPPI RIVER

NORTH

SOUTH

0 25 50 75 100
scale of miles

The river of America's heartland became a battleground and its banks bristled with guns. From Island No.10 to New Orleans at the mouth of the Mississippi, the jaws of the Union clamped down on the rebellious South.

The Confederacy's last chance to control the mighty river was at the citadel high atop the bluffs: Vicksburg. It finally fell to General Grant's Union troops after a six-week siege, July 4, 1863. The war for the river ended at Port Hudson four days later.

VICKSBURG

NATCHEZ falls May 18, 1863

PORT HUDSON

BATON ROUGE

July 8, 1863

NEW ORLEANS surrendered to Rear Admiral David G. Farragut of the U.S. Navy May 1, 1862.

He captured Baton Rouge May 12, 1862.

As he rode the westbound stage, Sam was delighted to see "the swift phantom of the desert": a Pony Express rider pounding away with the U. S. mail and news of the war back East. Orion began his government job and Sam took up silvermining and news reporting in the Nevada Territory. Sam had a way of telling more than just the facts, though, which led to his writing funny stories such as "The Celebrated Jumping Frog of Calaveras County" for newspapers in San Francisco, Sacramento, and Virginia City in the Nevada Territory.

The most famous humorist of the day had a pen name: Artemus Ward. So Sam tried out a few for himself: "Josh," "Rambler," and "Thomas Jefferson Snodgrass." On February 2, 1863, Sam signed a story "Mark Twain," a river term meaning two fathoms (twelve feet) deep. The name stuck.

Mark Twain earned a reputation as a comic lecturer when he was traveling correspondent to the Sandwich Islands, now known as Hawaii. He invented advertisements like this to get crowds of people to come to his first Sandwich Island Lecture, in San Francisco, on October 2, 1866:

MAGNIFICENT FIREWORKS

WERE IN CONTEMPLATION FOR THIS OCCASION, BUT THE IDEA WAS ABANDONED.

MR. MARK TWAIN
will deliver a
Serio~Humorous Lecture:
OUR FELLOW SAVAGES of the SANDWICH ISLANDS

THE CELEBRATED BEARDED WOMAN
IS NOT WITH THIS CIRCUS.

The Doors open at 7. The Trouble begins at 8!

While Mark Twain was making his name out West, big things were happening back on the old river: things he'd be writing about later on.

In the first forty years of steam on the Mississippi, more than four thousand people were killed or injured when boats sank, burned, or the boilers exploded. "Many people were flung considerable distances . . . shrieks and groans filled the air," is what grieving Sam wrote about the steamboat explosion that killed his own little brother, Henry, in the summer of 1858.

A terrible disaster, the worst ever, struck on April 27, 1865, near Memphis, Tennessee, just after the end of the Civil War. The boilers blew up on the *Sultana*, overloaded with Union soldiers on their way home. At least 1,547 people were killed, more than would be lost on the ocean liner *Titanic* forty-seven years later.

Never had steamboats been as luxurious as the *Mistress of the Mississippi*: the **J.M.White**. She had stained-glass windows and cut-glass chandeliers.

In spite of the terrible things that could happen, people still liked to see how fast a steamboat could go. "Racing was royal fun," said Mark Twain. "A race between two notoriously fleet steamers was an event of vast importance," as in the most famous steamboat race of all when the *Rob't. E. Lee* met the *Natchez* at the starting point in New Orleans, Thursday afternoon, June 30, 1870.

The fireboxes roared their hottest with wood, coal, tar, turpentine—even rotten meat and fatty bacon—to build up as much steam as possible. The sweaty crew prayed the boilers would hold together and the stripped-down boats wouldn't blow up. The *Rob't. E. Lee* made it to the finish line in St. Louis on the Fourth of July, in three days, eighteen hours, fourteen minutes: over three hours ahead of the *Natchez*. The *Lee* won the right to the prized golden deer antlers to sparkle high over the pilothouse between the smokestacks.

Never had steamboats been so big:
the Grand Republic was 350 feet long.

Not long before the great race of 1870, thirty-four-year-old Sam had gotten married. As time passed, Sam and Olivia had a son named Langdon who died when he was a baby, and three daughters: Susy, Clara, and Jean. They lived in a big house in Hartford, Connecticut. It looked a little bit like a steamboat.

In his middle years, Sam was still the same man, but different now: Mark Twain had become a star.

Puffing on a cigarette, he'd imagine for his audience a show at the Roman Colosseum: "NEW LIONS! NEW GLADIATORS! Box office now open!" he joked and drawled through passages from his popular travel books such as *Roughing It*, and his first best-seller, *Innocents Abroad*, published in 1869.

Across the country, cigars, collars, and sewing machines were named after him; there was even a dance called the Mark Twain Mazurka. Sam himself invented the self-pasting Mark Twain Patent Scrapbook. But probably his greatest invention was Mark Twain.

Mark Twain's best books were based on his boyhood in Hannibal, Missouri, on the banks of the Mississippi. Children as well as grown-ups loved to read about Tom, Huck, and Jim in *The Adventures of Huckleberry Finn* (1884).

"You don't know about me, without you have read a book by the name of *The Adventures of Tom Sawyer* [1875], but that ain't no matter. That book was made by Mr. Mark Twain, and he told the truth, mainly," said Huckleberry Finn. Before this, boys like raggedy Huck, an outsider, didn't get to talk in books. Because of these books, which made some people mad because of the way Huck talked, Mark Twain became more than just a celebrity. He was one of America's very best writers.

At St. Louis, Missouri, on the Fourth of July, 1874, President Ulysses S. Grant opened a marvel: the 6,220 feet long steel-arched EADS BRIDGE. It was built by the self-taught engineer JAMES EADS who had also designed the "ironclad" UNION gunboats. The bridge took seven years and cost $10,000,000.

Sam returned to his river, as a famous passenger, in 1882, to complete his book, *Life on the Mississippi*. He saw many changes since his piloting days. Same old river, but different now.

The Mississippi bristled with bridges. At the St. Louis levee, he saw "half a dozen sound-asleep steamboats where I used to see a solid mile of wide-awake ones! This was melancholy, this was woeful." Railroads were fast connecting the country in every direction, so the great passenger steamboats, the *grandes dames* who once ruled the river were no longer needed for transportation. But like Mark Twain, the Queens of the Mississippi had, in their heyday, put on quite a show.

"Mississippi steamboating was born about 1812; at the end of thirty years it had grown to mighty proportions; and in less than thirty years more it was dead: A strangely short life for so majestic a creature."

FROM **LIFE ON THE MISSISSIPPI**

In the last years of his life, Sam lost so much money on inventions and schemes to get rich that he went broke. Mark Twain, sixty years old, set out on a world lecture tour in 1895 to earn back his riches. Although he still made people laugh, and he was still honored and admired around the world, he was lonely, and sometimes gloomy and bitter. Olivia and two of their daughters were dead. He took to wearing white suits, partly to attract attention (it worked), and partly "to be clean in a dirty world."

Just as in the river, he sensed dangers beneath the shiny surfaces: He was pessimistic. But then, wrote Sam, "Everyone is a moon and has a dark side which he never shows to anybody." When Halley's comet returned to the night sky, Sam felt his life was coming to an end. His heart was weak. He could read the currents as well as ever. Sam died when he was seventy-four years old, in the spring, the river high in its banks, April 21, 1910.

Time and the wide, muddy Mississippi rolled on. These days, far downstream from Sam's days, millions of tons of coal, oil, potatoes, steel, stone, and grain, on barges pushed by diesel-powered tugboats, move up and down the river, past the bluffs, the flood plains, and concrete cities.

Long freight trains snake down the railroads. Cars and trucks zoom on the highways over and along the old river of driftwood and catfish. The Mississippi has been earnestly reorganized with locks, dams, levees, spillways, reservoirs, and pumps, but it can still flood chocolate-colored water all over the place. The rivercraft pass along a dredged-out, beacon-lit shipping channel that would amaze even the stoniest steamboat pilot. High overhead is the thin white trail of a jet. Same river, but different now.

"It was kind of solemn, drifting down the big still river,
laying on our backs looking up at the stars..."
—**Huckleberry Finn**

BIBLIOGRAPHY

ANDRIST, RALPH K. *The Mississippi*. Mahwah, NJ: Troll Associates, 1962.

BATES, ALAN L. *The Western Rivers Steamboat Cyclopoedium*. Leonia, NJ: Hustle Press, 1968.

HOLLING, HOLLING CLANCY. *Minn of the Mississippi*. Boston, MA: Houghton Mifflin Company, 1951.

RAY SAMUEL, L.V. HUBER, AND W.C. OGDEN. *Tales of the Mississippi*. Gretna, LA: Pelican Publishing Company, 1955.

WATKINS, T. H. *Mark Twain's Mississippi*. Palo Alto, CA: American West Publishing Co., 1974.